Elmer
and the
Kangaroo

DAVID McKEE

lishers

Elmer, the patchwork elephant, had just started his morning walk when Tiger arrived.

"Elmer," he said, "there's a stranger around, and he's acting very strangely. First he jumps, then he falls over."

"Strangers often act strangely," said Elmer. "That's why they're strangers."

"Well, I don't think he's happy," said Tiger.

Just then Lion appeared. "Hello, Elmer. Hello, Tiger," he said.
"Elmer, there's a strange chap around. He sort of . . . sort of . . ."
"Jumps," said Tiger. "Elmer knows."

"And then he kind of . . . well, he . . ."
"Falls over," finished Tiger. "Elmer knows."
"Yes, well, he also seems . . . ah . . ."
"Unhappy," said Tiger. "Elmer knows."
"Let's just go and see," said Elmer kindly.

Soon they came to a clearing. "This is where he usually jumps," said Tiger.

"And falls over," added Lion. "And here he comes."

A kangaroo jumped into the clearing. Then he stopped, fell over, picked himself up, and sobbed, "I'm a failure!"

"Not a happy chappy," said Lion.

"Let's talk to him," said Elmer.

"Hello," said Elmer. "What's the matter?"

"Hello," Kangaroo sniffed. "I can't jump. When I try to, I fall over. There's a jumping contest tomorrow, and I came here to practice, secretly. But I *can't* jump. I'll be laughed at."

"But you were jumping beautifully," said Tiger.

"Oh no, I was just bouncing along getting ready to jump. I'm a good bouncer," said Kangaroo, and to prove it he bounced higher than Giraffe, who happened to be passing.

"Very impressive," said Tiger.

"But when I think about jumping, I fall over," sighed Kangaroo.

"This needs some thought," said Elmer. "We'll be back tomorrow."

On the way home, Lion said, "Elmer, I know I'm a bit slow, but isn't a bounce a kind of jump?"

"Yes, Lion," said Elmer. "But Kangaroo thinks that a jump is something more difficult, more important. Like sometimes if you think about going to sleep, you can't, but when you don't think about it, you soon drop off."

The next morning, after talking to Lion and Tiger, Elmer went to meet Kangaroo.

"Come on, Kangaroo," he said. "Lion and Tiger will be by the river."

Elmer set off at a steady pace while Kangaroo bounced behind him, in front of him, around him, even over him.

When they got to the river, Lion and Tiger were on the other side, where Elmer had told them to wait.

"Drat!" said Elmer. "We'll get our feet wet."

Kangaroo laughed. Then, with an enormous bounce, he flew over the river and landed beside Lion and Tiger.

"Fantastic jump," said Tiger.

"You mean bounce," said Kangaroo. "I can't jump."

Lion chuckled. "But a bounce *is* a jump."

"Lion is right," said Elmer. "Forget about jumping. Just bounce. Now, let's go to that contest."

Kangaroo led the way, delighted that his new friends were going with him. They arrived just as the contest began.

After a while, Elmer said, "Come on, Kangaroo.
It's time you had a go."
Just then there was a roar of applause as a white
kangaroo made an enormous jump.
"That will be hard to beat," said Kangaroo.

Elmer whispered to Lion and Tiger, who went to stand just past the spot where the white kangaroo had landed.

As Kangaroo was getting ready, Elmer said, "Drat! We'll get our feet wet."

Kangaroo laughed. Then, with an enormous bounce, he landed once again right beside Lion and Tiger. And that was the winning jump.

Later, Kangaroo thanked Elmer, Lion, and Tiger for their help.
"You made me remember the river," he said, "instead of thinking
about jumping."

"Strange thing," Lion said when they were back home.
"At the contest, I felt that we were the . . . ah . . ."
"Strangers," finished Tiger.
"Yes," said Elmer. "And now we're all . . . ah . . ."
"FRIENDS!" they all laughed together.

For Fabio B and Amy Z

Elmer and the Kangaroo
Copyright © 2000 by David McKee
First published in Great Britain by Andersen Press, Ltd.
under the title *Elmer and the Stranger.*
Printed in Italy. All rights reserved.
http://www.harperchildrens.com

CIP information is on file at the Library of Congress.

1 2 3 4 5 6 7 8 9 10
❖
First Edition
This book has been printed on acid-free paper.